The Shelf Elf Helps Out

Jackie Mims Hopkins

Illustrated by Rebecca McKillip Thornburgh

Fort Atkinson, Wisconsin

Published by UpstartBooks
W5527 State Road 106
P.O. Box 800
Fort Atkinson, Wisconsin 53538-0800
1-800-448-4887

Text © 2006 by Jackie Mims Hopkins
Illustrations © 2006 by Rebecca McKillip Thornburgh

To my wonderful husband, Jeff, the "Top Shelf Elf" in my life and library.
Thank you to my rhyming buddies, Bobbie McDonald,
Dolores Lopez, and Ruth Wiesmann.

—J. M. H.

For Andrew and Annie Kammer, two of my
very favorite people, with love!

—R. McK. T.

hew, what a busy day in the library!

Just look at all of these books that need to go
back on the shelves.

I'm sure Ms. Turner, the librarian, would appreciate some help
shelving them.

I used to help the shoemaker and his
wife every night.

Tonight, I will help Ms. Turner
by putting these books back
where they belong.

 o you see the little sticker on the spine of this book?

It's called a call number and it is like an address.

It shows me where the book belongs on the shelf.

tacks, the Grand Dewey Daddy shelf elf, explains it like this.

The shelves in a library are like neighborhoods, and each book's address tells you in which neighborhood the book belongs.

 here are usually three kinds of call numbers, or addresses.

Picture books have an "E" on their spines,

chapter books have an "F" or "F-i-c,"

and the other books have numbers on them.

Most of the books with numbers are informational or nonfiction. That means they are about real people, places, things, and animals.

MELVIL·E·DEWEY

A long time ago, a man named Melvil Dewey came up with a way to organize books into ten groups.

Then he gave each group a special number from 000 to 999.

Follow me and I'll show you a few of the different kinds of books in each group.

In this neighborhood the addresses start at 000 and end at 099.

Encyclopedias, books about computers, and books about unexplained things like flying saucers are found here.

This book about the Loch Ness Monster goes on this shelf.

The zero hundreds is the place to look,

For encyclopedias or a Bigfoot book.

ere's a book about friendship.

Its address is in the 100s.

If you want to learn about friends or find books about feelings, you're in the right neighborhood.

The 100s books explain feelings you've had,

From happy to grumpy or even sad.

 his Noah's Ark book goes in the 200s neighborhood.

Books about different religions are in this section. There are also stories called myths. A myth is an imaginary story about gods, goddesses, or superhuman beings.

The 200s have religious books to read,

Or myths and legends, if that is what you need.

T he next shelf has books with 300s on their spines.

Choose one of these books to find out why we have holidays and other celebrations.

My Shelf Elf Book of Library Etiquette would belong on this shelf because there are books about manners here, too.

The 300s books tell of holidays,

And how we celebrate in many ways.

hile we are in the 300s neighborhood, I want to show you my favorite section—the 398s.

This shelf has fairy tales, tall tales, and folktales.

If you read "The Shoemaker and the Elves," you can find out about the job I had before I became a shelf elf.

The 398s have stories to thrill,

From Cinderella to Pecos Bill.

earn about languages by reading books from the 400s.

Check out a sign language book from this shelf to learn how to talk with your hands.

On the 400s shelf, languages abound.

Books about Spanish or French can be found.

f you like math and science,
this is the neighborhood for you.

Planets, wild animals, dinosaurs, and
experiments are just a few of the
subjects in this section.

The 500s shelf
is the place
to explore,

Science,
math,
or a dinosaur.

 irplanes, cars, and pets are the favorites in the 600s neighborhood. I like reading the books about pets.

I keep looking for a book about pet bookerpillars, but I haven't found one yet.

The 600s books are your best bets,

For airplanes, cars, and friendly pets.

This football book belongs on the 700s shelf.

All sports, art, and music books are in this neighborhood, too.

The 700s shelf has books of all sorts,

For drawing, music, and even sports.

 hy did the chicken cross the road?

You can find out in one of the joke or riddle books in the 800s.

Or, you might want to have some fun with rhyming words in the poetry books found in this neighborhood.

The 800s is the place to be,

For jokes, riddles, and poetry.

ooks in the 900s take you places.

You can learn interesting facts about the states in America or find out about countries far away.

There are also books about history. These books help us learn what happened a long time ago.

In the 900s there's geography,

People, places, and history.

ARMSTRONG

Dr. M. Curie

DI MAGGIO

HENRY VIII

GENGHIS KHAN

LINCOLN

NAPOLEON

SKOOB

SOJOURNER TRUTH

YAMAGUCHI

he last book that needs to be shelved is about Abraham Lincoln.

This book about his life is called a biography.

Some libraries put a "B" on the spine, and some put on the Dewey number "92," but either address tells you this is a book about a real person's life.

If the address says 92 or B, You have found a biography.

 inally, the book cart is empty and I'm ready to relax and read!

Did you see a book neighborhood you would like to visit?

If you can't remember the neighborhoods where your favorite kinds of books are, just ask your librarian to help you.

And now, for a little rest …

an alien spaceship
Anubis
an apple car

atlas
an Aztec temple
Baba Yaga's chicken hut
a ballerina
a banana peel
a banjo
a basket of yarn
beetles
a birthday cake
bowling pins
a broom
a bug car
building blocks
a bust of Plato

a frog prince
a grandfather clock
a hairy paw
a harp

a hatching chick
Hermes
a hopscotch game
Humpty Dumpty

a pagoda
a paintbrush
a Parcheesi board
the Parthenon

Paul Bunyan and Babe
Pecos Bill

a camera
a canoe
a checker board
chess pieces
a Chinese dragon
Cinderella's slipper
a clothesline
a clown car
a conch shell
a cornucopia
a dancing fish
a domino
a double helix
an easel
the Eiffel Tower
a fish skeleton
a fisherman
the formula for a normal distribution

Jack and the Beanstalk
a jack-o-lantern
a juggler
a knock-knock door
a ladder
a leprechaun
Little Miss Muffet
the Loch Ness monster
a magnet
a marching band
a menorah
a mermaid
a mitten
a Model T Ford
a molecule model

Pegasus
a pencil
a penguin

a phrenology model
a playing card
a pocket watch
a potatohead man
a pumpkin coach
a puppy pilot
Rodin's "The Thinker"
a rubber ducky
a saw
a sculptor
the seven dwarfs
a shepherd
a skier
a soccer ball
a spider web
a spool of thread
a starfish
a suitcase

a teacup car
a telescope
a tennis racket
The Three Bears
The Three Billy Goats Gruff
Thumbelina
a toothbrush
The Tortoise and the Hare
a tuning fork
an umbrella
a violin
a water faucet
Wee Willie Winkie
a windup car
a witch's candy cottage

Mother Goose
a nutcracker
The Owl and the Pussycat

Or not!

Before I put away this new pile of books,
see if you can find all of these things for me—
I know they're somewhere in the pages of this book!